The Groaning Ghost

First published in 2009
by Wayland

This paperback edition published in 2010 by Wayland

Text copyright © Liss Norton 2009
Illustration copyright © Emma McCann 2009

Wayland
338 Euston Road
London NW1 3BH

Wayland Australia
Level 17/207 Kent Street
Sydney, NSW 2000

The rights of Liss Norton to be identified as the Author
and Emma McCann to be identified as the Illustrator of this Work have
been asserted by them in accordance with the Copyright, Designs and
Patents Act, 1988.

Series Editor: Louise John
Editor: Katie Powell
Cover design: Paul Cherrill
Design: D.R.ink
Consultant: Shirley Bickler

A CIP catalogue record for this book is available from the British Library.

ISBN 9780750257343 (hbk)
ISBN 9780750260305 (pbk)

Printed in China

Wayland is a division of Hachette Children's Books,
an Hachette UK Company

www.hachette.co.uk

The Groaning Ghost

Written by Liss Norton
Illustrated by Emma McCann

WAYLAND

Fergus the Superfrog was playing hopscotch with his best friend, Doris, when he heard a strange noise. Someone sounded very upset.

5

Fergus pulled on his red suit, his red helmet with the yellow stripe, and his matching red rocket boots.

Then he and Doris flew off
to investigate.

A ghost, dressed in old-fashioned clothes, was sitting on a fallen tree and groaning very loudly.

"Woo-hoo!" he wailed.

Doris flew down next to the ghost.
"What's the matter?" she asked.

"My house is being knocked down," groaned the ghost. "I'm Sir Mortimer Fortimer, and I've lived in Fortimer House for 500 years."

"Fergus can help save your house!"
said Doris.

Fergus and Doris followed Mortimer to Fortimer House. It was a huge house with an overgrown garden. Next to the house was a round, muddy lake.

A man was driving a yellow digger towards the house.

"Try scaring the driver," suggested Doris. "He might be afraid of ghosts."

Sir Mortimer glided towards the digger driver, waving his arms in the air. "Woo-hoo!" he wailed. "Leave my home alone!"

"I'm not scared of ghosts!" said the digger driver. "Ghosts can only wail and walk through walls. They aren't scary!"

And, with that, he drove the digger
nearer to the house.

"He isn't afraid of me," Sir Mortimer wailed. "Can you do anything, Superfrog?"

"Let's all scare him," croaked Fergus. "Three ghosts are much scarier than one."

Fergus and Doris flew into the
house through a broken window.
In the attic they found some
dusty old sheets.

Fergus and Doris put the sheets over their heads and zoomed out of the chimney.
"Woo-hoo," they wailed.
"Gooooo away!"

The digger driver was getting angry. "Three ghosts are no more scary than one," he said. "Get out of my way. Nothing can scare me!"

"We'll see about that!" Fergus
shouted, pulling off his sheet.

Fergus flew towards the digger and, summoning all of his Superfrog strength, he lifted it off the ground.

"Put me down!" shouted the digger driver as he rose up into the air. "I'm terrified of heights! Someone help me!"

Fergus ignored the driver and carried the digger round to the side of the house. With a big heave-ho, he threw it into the lake.

It landed with a big splash!

The digger driver sat in the muddy water. "You've ruined my digger!" he shouted.

"Serves you right," said Fergus.

Sir Mortimer and Doris flew towards him, clapping and cheering.

"Fergus, you saved the day!" said Doris.

"Thank you, Fergus," Sir Mortimer said. "Now I can return home."

And, with a wave, he walked straight through the wall.

"Ghosts seem to have superpowers, too!" laughed Doris.

START READING is a series of highly enjoyable books for beginner readers. **The books have been carefully graded to match the Book Bands widely used in schools.** This enables readers to be sure they choose books that match their own reading ability.

Look out for the Band colour on the book in our Start Reading logo.

The Bands are:

Pink Band 1A & 1B

Red Band 2

Yellow Band 3

Blue Band 4

Green Band 5

Orange Band 6

Turquoise Band 7

Purple Band 8

Gold Band 9

START READING books can be read independently or shared with an adult. They promote the enjoyment of reading through satisfying stories supported by fun illustrations.

Liss Norton used to be a teacher. She now writes books, musicals and plays for children. She is keen on growing organic fruit and veg at her allotment, on her granddaughters, Maddie and Arabella, and on visiting castles. One day she hopes to find a secret passage...

Emma McCann is currently living a dual life. By day, she is a mild-mannered illustrator, but by night she becomes the masked crime-fighter and master cake-baker "Red Velvet". She hopes to be joined soon in her crime fighting/cake baking adventures by a small, dog-shaped partner.